The Little Train Set
Billy the hero!

ISBN: 978-0-9927317-3-1

The Little Train Set

Billy the hero!

By

Michael K Chapman

Dedication

This book is dedicated to Alex and Kenneth for their
roles in the life of
The Little Train Set.

Other titles in The Little Train Set series:

Someone is missing!

Chapter One: The Little Train Set.

There is a little train set that sits upon a board. There are houses and a church, there is even a school. There are lots of roads with cars and a garage too. The green grass and trees looked almost real. There are shops and a bank and a playground too, everything one could wish for in a little train set on a board.

The shops and church.

A young boy plays with the train set, his granddad built for him. It used to be his uncles but now it is his. The little boy loves the train set that granddad built. The trains all run on tiny tracks. A diesel train pulls the passengers and two small steam engines carry the goods and cargo. The little steam engines carry all kinds of things around the little train set. They sometimes carry cars and sometimes little boxes that look like real cargo containers, but mostly little bits and pieces that the young boy can fit into the little train trucks.

There are two stations on the train set, one on either side. The biggest station has a signal box, a large waiting room and toilets. The small station also has a waiting room but this one is much smaller with an open front. A newspaper hut sits beside the small waiting room on the small platform.

The Little Station.

The passenger train runs right around the little train set that sits on a board. It goes under the shops through a tunnel. It stops at the big station with its signal box, waiting room and toilets before carrying on through the train yard. The passenger train keeps going around, from the train yard, past the little school and stops at the small platform with the small waiting room and the tiny newspaper hut. Then the passenger train goes into the tunnel once again to chug around the little train set once more.

The Passenger Train

The train set is busy, with houses, cars and trains but wait, where are all the people? There are no people living in the houses or riding the trains. No people visiting the shops or driving their cars. Whatever could have happened to the people? The boy saw the train set was still, people on the little train set would make it seem alive and real. He wished so hard that the little train set would be alive. So one day he asked his granddad if he could put some people on the little train set and granddad said he would.

The little boy waited, he played with the trains and he played with the cars. He moved freight and bits and pieces with the Blue engine and he drove the passenger train around the little train set and its town. The boy had decided to call the little town, Little Town. After all he thought, it is a little train set with a little town. He thought the name was very clever.

The Blue Engine.

Then one day while the young boy was visiting his grandparents, his wish came true and he found his granddad had filled the little train set with lots of little people. Suddenly the little train set, with shops and a church, with trains and with cars now had people as well! Lots of little people were spread over the little train set, people and children to live in the houses and go to the school. The people can visit the shops and ride the trains. The little train set was complete.

The young boy played with the train set and its new people for hours, moving the people around the shops and the town, onto the two train stations and some even went to church. The boy picked out the bank manager and the shop keepers. He chose the vicar for the church and he placed people on the platforms. He even put little people in the garage and around the school. He was a happy little boy and he was pleased with his little train set.

People on the Little Train Set.

The people looked almost real on the train set and the little boy began to imagine them coming to life. In fact he wished so hard that his little town and its little railway was alive.

Sadly the time came for the little boy to go home with his mum and his baby sister. That evening he left his little train set that sat upon a board, he turned off the light and closed the spare room door. His grandparents saw the boy and his mum and his sister to their car and waved as the car started and began the journey home.

That night while tucked up in his bed, the sleepy boy wished and wished that he could play with his little train set again. He wished and wished that the trains and the cars could move by themselves and he wished and wished that all the little people in Little Town were real. But he knew deep down inside of him that this could never happen, toys do not come to life, do they?

The little boy fell asleep and dreamed about his little train set.

The empty streets.

Chapter Three: Billy the banker's son

The Little Town had its own bank and of course the bank had a bank manager. Billy's dad was the banker manager. He looked after everyone's money and even lent money to some people. He looked after people's important things, locked up tight in his bank. Looking after a bank is a very important job and Billy's dad worked hard. But at weekends, when the bank was closed, Billy and his dad had another job. A job they both loved very much. Every weekend, Billy and his dad helped to run the station and all the trains of Little Town.

The Banker and his son, Billy.

One Saturday when the bank was closed, Billy and his dad went off to work with the trains. Today the Red engine was going to take a large cargo container around the town. Billy and his dad were ready to help as they stood on the small station. They were there to help make sure everything was well. In the distance Billy could hear the Red engine puffing towards him. He liked the Red engine, it was very old and not very fast but it was pretty with its bright red paint work. Slowly the Red engine came closer to the small station where Billy stood.

The Red Engine.

Suddenly there came a loud noise like metal scratching on metal. The Red engine came to a shaky stop almost beside Billy on the small station. Billy knew the Red engine had broken down because it broke down quite a lot. But now Billy was worried. The big passenger train was due to come through the small station very soon and there might be a crash!

What could Billy and his dad do? Billy knew he had to help the Red engine before it was hurt in the crash, but what could he do? Billy looked around the little train set and saw who could help. It was the Blue engine! It was on one of the sidings and not too far away. As fast as they could, Billy and his dad ran down the small station and over to the train yard where the Blue engine sat puffing gently on its rails.

Chapter four: A brave Engine

'Help!' called Billy as he neared the quiet Blue engine. 'The Red engine has broken down and the passenger train is coming!'

The Blue engine roared its engine into life, 'I can help. I will pull the Red engine and the cargo. I am fast and strong, I can do it!'

'Let's go then,' called Billy's dad, 'if we are quick we can go round the town in the opposite direction to the passenger train, but we will need to go very fast.'

'I am fast! I can do it. I can save the Red engine!' sang the Blue engine as it built up steam.

Billy and his dad jumped onto the Blue engine and held on tight, Billy also held on tight to his hat. He knew the Blue engine was fast!

With a cloud of steam the Blue engine spun its wheels and reversed out of the siding where it had stood. It reversed out of the train yard and the work sheds, it reversed around the bend and on towards the main line. Billy held on tightly as the Blue engine raced in reverse, he also kept a hold of his hat. The Blue engine rushed backwards around the track, crossing onto the main line seconds after the passenger train had flashed past. Past the big station and into the tunnel sped the Blue engine, through the long dark tunnel that ran under the shops and out into the light once more. The Blue engine had reached the small station. The Blue engine stopped so quickly, Billy almost did lose his hat, for there just ahead on the line was the Red engine and the truck with its cargo.

The Red Engine and the truck with its cargo.

The poor broken Red engine looked sad as it stood lonely next to the small station, a thin trickle of steam rising from its funnel. Billy was afraid for the Red engine because he could hear the passenger train coming, and it was coming fast. If it crashed into the Red engine and its truck carrying the cargo, it would surely knock the Red engine right off the tracks!

Billy's dad jumped down from the Blue engine and ran as fast as he could to hook up the two trains together. Billy stayed on the Blue engine as it gently reversed up to the Red engine. Billy's dad waited to hook the two engines together. When the Blue engine stopped, Billy jumped down from the Blue engine and ran up onto the small station. He could run very fast and he ran as fast as he could. Billy was worried he might get in the way and be hurt, but he felt safe once he was on the platform of the small station.

He could hear the mighty passenger train coming closer. It was almost around the bend that led into the small station. With shaking hands Billy's dad quickly hooked the Blue engine onto the broken Red engine.

Hooking the two trains together.

Billy's dad had to leap out of the way as the Blue engine began to move forward, pulling both the Red engine and the truck with its cargo. It moved so slowly Billy was sure it was going to be too late. As the passenger train loomed closer, Billy's dad leapt with all his might up onto the platform beside Billy and away from the oncoming crash.

The Passenger train is coming!

The Blue engine began to move forward, facing the way back along the track. The Blue engine began to pull faster. Faster and faster it chuffed, pulling the Red engine and its truck with the cargo away from the small platform. The brave Blue engine pulled harder and harder as it tried its very best to save its friend, the Red engine.

Billy did not know if the Blue engine was going to be fast enough, he could see the passenger train speeding around the bend. Would there be a crash? If there was a crash now, all three trains could be hurt, the brave Blue engine, the broken Red engine and the mighty passenger train. Oh how Billy worried as still the Blue engine pulled with all its strength.

The two trains finally move from the station.

At last Billy could see that the two little engines were moving into the tunnel, they were going to make it away before the passenger train reached the small station. Happily Billy watched the brave Blue engine pull the broken Red engine and its truck with the cargo and disappear into the tunnel under the shops. Seconds later the mighty passenger train rolled into the small station and came to a halt beside the platform, just as it always did. The Passenger train pulls into the small station.

The passenger train stopped at both the

big station and the small station to let its passengers on or off.

Chapter Five: Safe.

The brave little Blue engine pulled the broken Red engine and its truck with the cargo safely round the little train set and off onto a siding for repair. The Blue engine was very tired but very happy. The Blue engine had saved the broken Red engine and the truck. The Blue engine had saved the cargo and the passenger train all in one go.

Later Billy and his dad went to where the Blue engine rested in the work shed and said thank you to the Blue engine. The Blue engine replied that it was the quick thinking of Billy that really saved the day.

The Red Engine in the repair shed.

Finally after such an exciting day helping on the little railway, Billy and his dad went home. Tomorrow was Sunday and Billy's dad would see his friend the Vicar at church. But now it was time for Billy to go home and to bed. He was very tired but very happy that there had not been a train crash in Little Town.

The Vicar waiting outside his church.

So there were two hero's that day in the young boy's dream and when he awoke in the morning, he told his mum all about his dream. Later that week when the boy went to his grandparents for tea, the boy told the dream to his granddad. His granddad was pleased that the engines and train did not crash and no one was hurt. Granddad promised to try and repair the Red engine but it is old and slow, 'just like me' said granddad. After tea the boy and his granddad went off to the spare room to play with the little train set. The little boy wondered what stories about the little train set he would dream next . . . .

The End

(for a little while)

39567599R00018

Made in the USA
Charleston, SC
10 March 2015